The Boxcar Children Mysteries

THE MYSTERY IN SAN FRANCISCO

created by

GERTRUDE CHANDLER WARNER

Illustrated by Charles Tang

SCHOLASTIC INC.
New York Toronto London Auckland Sydney

ISBN 0-590-64926-4

Copyright © 1997 by Albert Whitman & Company. All rights reserved. Published by Scholastic Inc., 555 Broadway, New York, NY 10012 by arrangement with Albert Whitman & Company. THE BOXCAR CHILDREN is a registered trademark of Albert Whitman & Company.

12 11 10 9 8   5 6 7 8 9/0

Printed in the U.S.A.   40

First Scholastic printing, February 1997

Contents

CHAPTER 1

The Arrival

"There he is!" said six-year-old Benny.

The airport waiting room was crowded, but the Aldens all saw the man in the baseball cap.

Henry waved to him. "That's Uncle Andy, all right."

"But where's Aunt Jane?" Jessie said.

The Aldens had come to San Francisco to visit their grandfather's sister, Jane, and her husband, Andy Bean. Chattering excitedly, the children surrounded their uncle. He laughed as he hugged them.

"Where's Aunt Jane?" ten-year-old Violet asked.

"She had some shopping to do," Uncle Andy explained. "She's going to meet us for lunch."

Benny nodded. "Good," he said. "I'm hungry."

"We ate on the plane," twelve-year-old Jessie reminded her brother.

"But Jessie, that was hours ago," said Benny.

Uncle Andy laughed. "Same old Benny," he teased. Then he said, "Let's get your luggage."

Fourteen-year-old Henry held up his duffel bag. "We carried everything on the plane with us," he said.

Benny pointed over his shoulder. "All my stuff is in my backpack."

"Well, then, let's go," Uncle Andy said.

On the way to the parking garage, he asked, "Did you have a nice trip?"

The Aldens said, "Yes!"

"I think you'll enjoy San Francisco," their uncle told them. "It's an interesting city."

He and Aunt Jane had been staying in San Francisco for the last few weeks. They would not return home until Uncle Andy had finished his business here.

"We're happy you invited us," Violet said.

Uncle Andy smiled. "We're happy to have you," he said. "I hope you've thought about what you want to do."

"We each want to do something different," Jessie said.

Henry nodded. "I'd like to see Chinatown. I've been reading about it."

"I'd like to take a boat trip," Violet told him. She had heard about sightseeing boat tours.

"The Golden Gate Bridge is my choice," Jessie put in.

"And the cable cars!" Benny said. "Don't forget the cable cars. They remind me of our boxcar."

The Alden children used to live alone in a boxcar after their parents had died. Then their grandfather found them and took them to his beautiful home in Greenfield.

Uncle Andy nodded. "You'll see all that and more." He took out his car keys. "Here we are," he said, and opened the trunk.

The Aldens piled their luggage inside. Then they all climbed into the car.

"Where are we going?" Benny asked.

Uncle Andy started the engine. "To Fisherman's Wharf," he said. "It's a good place to begin our sightseeing."

The Aldens looked at one another and smiled. With so much to do, they knew this would be a special trip.

Before long, they were in the city. The sun shone brightly on the bay. The tall buildings seemed to sparkle. Uncle Andy drove up one steep hill and down another.

"San Francisco sure is hilly," Violet observed.

"Some people call it the City of Hills," Uncle Andy said.

The car crested a hill and started down.

"They should call it roller-coaster city," Benny said. Everyone laughed.

Soon Uncle Andy pulled into a parking space.

"There's Aunt Jane!" Violet said.

Benny was the first one out of the car. "Aunt Jane!" he called, and ran toward the woman. The other Aldens hurried after him. Aunt Jane held out her arms. Benny hugged her.

"I'm so glad to see you all!" Aunt Jane said.

"We're glad to see you, too," Jessie said.

"If it's okay with everyone, I thought we'd tour the pier first," Aunt Jane said, smiling. "That way we'll work up an appetite."

They strolled along the brick sidewalk and under a sign that read PIER 39. The place was buzzing with activity. Here, an artist sketched a visitor. There, a group posed for a photo. Everywhere, people wandered along the wooden plank walkway. They went in and out of the small shops that lined both sides of the pier.

In one shop, Violet said, "We should buy

a souvenir for Soo Lee." Seven-year-old Soo Lee was the Aldens' adopted cousin.

"I'm surprised she didn't come with you," Uncle Andy said.

"She wanted to come," Jessie explained, "but she's playing her violin in a concert this week."

"She's a really good violinist," Benny put in.

"Cousin Joe has been teaching her to play," Violet said.

"And Violet's been helping her practice," Henry added.

Aunt Jane nodded. "You children certainly know how to help people," she said. "Just like your grandfather."

"We should buy something for Grandfather, too," Jessie said. She held up a T-shirt. On the front was a picture of the Golden Gate Bridge. "Do you think he'd like this?"

"You'll be here a while," Uncle Andy said. "Why don't you wait to buy your gifts. We'll be seeing so much more."

At the far end of the pier, a carousel

whirled, its music playing. There were colorful horses on two levels.

Benny was impressed. "I've never seen a merry-go-round with an upstairs and a downstairs," he said.

Aunt Jane laughed. "How about a ride?" she said.

"Will you ride with us?" Jessie asked.

"Of course we will!" Uncle Andy answered.

The Aldens walked around the carousel. Each chose a horse to ride. Aunt Jane and Uncle Andy sat in a carriage shaped like Cinderella's. The music started and off they went. Up and down. Around and around. The bright colors along the pier streaked and blurred. Above them, the sky was like a blue dome.

When the ride was over, everyone felt wobbly. "Let's sit here until we get our land legs," Uncle Andy said, pointing to a nearby bench.

Henry said, "If we're like this from a ride on the merry-go-round, I wonder how we'd be after a ride in a boat."

"You'll soon see," Uncle Andy said. "And let me tell you, the water can be pretty choppy out in the bay."

After a few minutes, Aunt Jane stood up. "Let's take a look at the water right now," she said, and led the way to the far end of the pier.

The large, open deck was filled with people. Many of them had cameras. All of them were quiet as they looked out over the water. Far to the west, tall towers rose above the water.

"Is that the Golden Gate?" Jessie asked.

"That's right," Uncle Andy said. "It's one of the longest suspension bridges in the world."

The breeze picked up. It was chilly and damp and smelled of fish. After a while, Uncle Andy said, "Why don't we go have some lunch. I know just the place." He led them along the walk behind the shops. They heard a loud barking sound.

"What's that?" Violet asked.

"Look over the rail and you'll see," Aunt Jane told them.

Below them, sea lions lounged on large, floating platforms. Their thick, dark coats were shiny with sunlight. As the children watched, a few sea lions slipped into the water. Some stood on their back flippers and barked. Others slept through the commotion.

"I wish I had some bread or something to feed them," Benny said.

Jessie pointed to a sign. "It says don't feed the sea lions."

"They can take care of themselves," Uncle Andy said.

"Judging from the size of them, they have plenty to eat," Henry observed.

They continued along the way to a broad wooden staircase and climbed to the upper deck.

"The Eagle Café," Uncle Andy said. They went inside and took a table beside a large window.

Jessie looked around at the white walls and the green tables. "This place looks old," she said.

"It's the oldest place on the pier," Uncle

Andy said. He told them the restaurant's history.

While they waited for their lunch, they watched the boats bobbing in the water below them.

"Are those fishing boats?" Benny asked.

"Most are sailboats," Aunt Jane answered. "They tie up here."

Uncle Andy pointed to several smaller boats at the end of the dock. "Those few out there are fishing boats."

Aunt Jane said, "But most of the fishing boats are down several blocks."

After they had eaten a delicious lunch of hamburgers and french fries, Uncle Andy said, "We have a friend who owns a fishing boat. His name is Charlie. Let's walk along the wharf. Maybe we'll be able to find him."

They walked west. Pigeons waddled at their feet. Gulls flew overhead, dipping and diving.

They hadn't gone far when Uncle Andy said, "Oh, there's Charlie!"

A short, stocky man stood on a pier beside a small fishing boat. On the side of the blue and white boat were the words *Charlie's Chum*.

"That must be Charlie's boat," Violet said.

"It is," Andy said.

"Chum? Doesn't that mean friend?" Benny asked. "That's a strange name for a boat."

"Charlie's boat is like a friend to him," Aunt Jane said.

"Chum also means bait," Henry said.

Benny liked double meanings. "On second thought," he said, "that's a good name for a fishing boat."

They headed down the long pier toward Charlie. Aunt Jane waved. Charlie saw them. He did not wave back. And he was frowning.

"Charlie, what are you doing here?" Uncle Andy asked as they approached. "Aren't you usually docked down the way with the rest of the fishermen?"

Charlie nodded. "Herring season," he explained. "They were overcrowded. A few of us agreed to dock here."

"Charlie, I want you to meet my brother's grandchildren," Aunt Jane said. "They've been wanting to meet a fisherman."

Charlie glanced at the Aldens. He nodded a greeting, but he did not smile. "Good you met me today," he said. "I might not be a fisherman tomorrow."

Uncle Andy cocked his head to one side. "More trouble?" he asked.

Charlie didn't seem to hear the question. He looked over his shoulder. Henry followed his gaze. Not far away, a tall man in a dark suit and sunglasses leaned against a rail, staring at them. When Charlie caught his eye, he quickly looked away.

I wonder who that man is, Henry thought. *He sure doesn't seem dressed for a day at the pier.*

"We just toured Pier Thirty-nine," Aunt Jane said to Charlie, startling Henry out of his thoughts.

Charlie turned back to the Aldens. Shaking his head, he said, "Everybody wants to visit Pier Thirty-nine."

"We liked it a lot," Benny said.

"We've never seen anything quite like it," Jessie added.

"It's nothing but window dressing for the tourists," Charlie said. "Wait till you get a taste of the real wharf."

Down the way, a young woman called, "Charlie!" Her long, red hair glistened in the sunlight.

"I think someone's calling you," Violet said.

Charlie turned. "That's Kate Kerry," he said. "She's working for me and going to school, too. Putting herself through college." Then he added, "There're some fish I have to fry," and he hurried off without saying good-bye.

Puzzled, the Aldens watched him go.

"Charlie just isn't himself these days," Uncle Andy said as he shook his head.

CHAPTER 2

A Crooked Street

Uncle Andy suggested that they continue along the wharf. "I'll show you where Charlie usually docks."

They passed big sightseeing boats. Aunt Jane stopped at the ticket booths to collect information. "So we'll be prepared for our tour," she explained.

A block away, at open-air fish markets, men prepared giant crabs for steaming kettles. Inside, people sat at tables with checkered cloths enjoying fresh fish dishes.

They came to an open section. At the

railing, Uncle Andy said, "Look down there."

The Aldens looked over the side. Below them fishing boats — small and large — rocked beside high wooden posts. No docks separated the crafts.

"How do the fishermen get on their boats?" Violet asked.

Uncle Andy pointed out the metal ladders leading down to each boat.

"I can see why Charlie had to dock somewhere else," Benny observed. "This place is filled up."

Aunt Jane headed toward the car. "Let's go home," she said. "It's time you children were settled in."

Benny skipped after her. "Is your friend Charlie a fisherman *and* a cook?" he asked.

Uncle Andy opened the car door. "A cook? Charlie? What makes you think that, Benny?"

Benny climbed into the backseat. "He said he had to fry some fish."

Uncle Andy eased into the driver's seat. "That's just an expression," he said. After everyone was inside the car, Uncle Andy started the engine and soon they were on their way.

"I've never heard that expression before," Violet said. "About frying fish. What does it mean?"

"It means he has some business to take care of," Uncle Andy explained.

"What kind of business?" Benny asked.

"Fishermen lead busy lives," Aunt Jane answered. "They're out on the water before dawn, and when they come back to shore, they have to take care of their catch."

"I don't think Charlie was talking about ordinary business, though," Uncle Andy said. "There's been trouble on the wharf."

"Trouble?" Henry repeated. "What kind of trouble?"

Uncle Andy shrugged. "Charlie hasn't wanted to talk about it, but I know something is bothering him."

"That explains it," Benny said.

In the front seat, Aunt Jane turned to look at him. "Explains what, Benny?"

"Well, he wasn't very friendly."

"Benny, that's not polite," Violet said.

"It's okay, Violet. Benny's right," Uncle Andy said.

"That wasn't like Charlie at all," Aunt Jane said. "He must be very worried about something."

They slowed down. "Look to your left," Aunt Jane told them. "We rent the second house right down there."

The sign said LOMBARD STREET. Underneath it, the narrow road zigzagged down the hill. Houses and flower gardens were perched on either side. The Aldens were amazed.

"I've never seen such a crooked street," Henry said.

"And I doubt you'll ever see another one," Uncle Andy told him. "This block of Lombard Street is said to be the crookedest street in the world."

He pulled into a garage underneath a white house. Benny hopped out. "Don't go inside yet," Benny said. "I want to see something."

The others followed him. Then they

stood watching as Benny dashed down the brick street. He didn't go far, though, and after a few seconds, he came trudging toward them.

"Eight!" he said. "There are eight sharp turns!" He stopped to catch his breath.

Uncle Andy chuckled. "Much easier going down than coming up. Right, Benny?"

Inside, Aunt Jane showed them to their rooms. The boys had one, the girls another. Each room had a view of the bay below. They unpacked and then met on the deck outside their rooms. The view was thrilling.

Henry dug a guidebook out of his back pocket. He looked at a map. "See that tower?" he said. "It's called Coit Tower. It was built to look like a fire hose nozzle. It's a tribute to the firemen who fought the earthquake fires in 1906."

Benny shivered. "I hope there's no earthquake while we're here," he said.

Jessie said, "I've been thinking about Charlie. I wonder what could be bothering him."

"Maybe he didn't catch many fish today," Benny suggested.

"Fishermen are probably used to bad days," Violet said.

"Uncle Andy mentioned trouble," Henry said. "I saw a man on the wharf. He was acting strangely. I wonder if he has anything to do with the trouble."

"The one in the suit?" Jessie asked.

"I saw that man, too," Violet said.

"He seemed out of place," Henry said. "He was so dressed up."

Benny hadn't noticed the man. "Maybe he was sightseeing like us," he suggested.

Henry shook his head. "I don't think so."

"He was staring right at us," Violet said.

"At Charlie, not us," Jessie corrected.

"And when Charlie looked at him, he turned away," Henry said.

Benny smiled. "Great! Another mystery," he said. "I'm ready!"

By the time they came downstairs, Aunt Jane was preparing supper. "I thought we'd eat here in the kitchen tonight," she said.

"It looks like home," Benny said. He was thinking of Grandfather Alden's big, airy kitchen in Greenfield, where they all lived.

Henry offered to set the table. Aunt Jane showed him where she kept the plates and silverware.

"Is there anything we can help you with?" Jessie asked.

Aunt Jane said, "No, thank you. Everything's ready. We had such a big lunch, I wasn't sure what to fix. I decided on a little of this and a little of that."

She carried a large platter of meats and cheeses to the table. To that, she added a basket of bread, a bowl of fruit, and a pitcher of cold milk.

Benny rubbed his hands together. "I'll have a little of everything," he said. They made sandwiches and ate fruit. Benny drank two glasses of milk.

When they had finished eating, Jessie asked, "Do you know that woman — the one who works for Charlie?"

"Kate Kerry," Uncle Andy said. "We've

met her. She's been working for Charlie for a while. But I can't say we really *know* her."

"Why do you ask?" said Aunt Jane.

"I just wondered," Jessie said.

"Has she heard about the trouble Charlie's having?" Henry asked.

"I can't say for certain," Uncle Andy answered. "Charlie doesn't talk about it much."

"Charlie's not one to complain," Aunt Jane said.

Henry looked at his uncle. "Is Charlie the only one having trouble?"

Uncle Andy shook his head. "I don't think so."

When they were finished eating, the children cleared the table. Uncle Andy got out the maps so they could plan their next day.

"Refresh my memory," Uncle Andy said. "What was it you wanted to see?"

The Aldens all spoke at once. Aunt Jane held up her hands. "One at a time," she said.

"I have an idea," Uncle Andy said. He opened a drawer and took out paper and pencil. "Each of you write down what you most want to see."

Uncle Andy got his baseball cap from a hook near the back door. "Now, put the papers in my hat."

Each Alden dropped a folded piece of paper into the cap. "Now what?" Benny asked.

"Nothing yet," Uncle Andy answered. "We'll just leave this here." He put the cap on the counter near the phone. "Let everything sit till morning. Then I'll pick a paper. Where we go will be a surprise."

Aunt Jane smiled at her husband. "Andy Bean, you are full of good ideas."

The Aldens weren't so sure this was a good idea. They were so excited they didn't know if they could wait until morning to find out where they would go first.

"We'd better get to bed early," Andy suggested. "We want to be rested for whatever comes."

That did seem like a good idea. The sooner they went to sleep, the sooner morning would come. Upstairs, Benny said, "I'm too excited to sleep. I'll probably lie awake all night trying to figure out which place we'll see first."

The other Aldens smiled at one another. They knew Benny would soon be sound asleep.

CHAPTER 3

Sightseeing

First thing in the morning, Aunt Jane said, "Andy, here's your cap." She handed him the baseball cap containing the four slips of paper.

"Hurry, Uncle Andy!" Benny said.

The Aldens watched as Uncle Andy reached into the hat. He drew out a piece of paper and looked at it.

"What does it say?" Violet asked.

Uncle Andy smiled. "I think I'll keep it a surprise," he said, and put the paper in his pocket.

At first the Aldens were disappointed. They didn't want to wait another minute to find out where they were going.

Then Jessie said, "That's a good idea, Uncle Andy."

Henry agreed. "The longer the wait, the better the surprise."

"Let's get going!" Benny urged. "We can wait on the way."

Violet laughed. "What about breakfast, Benny?"

"Oh," Benny said. "I forgot."

They all laughed. It wasn't like Benny to forget about a meal.

"We'll eat breakfast out," Aunt Jane said. "I know the perfect place."

And off they went.

Clang! Clang! went the cable car as it came down the hill toward them. When it stopped, Uncle Andy said, "Hop on!"

"Watch your step!" the friendly conductor called out.

Benny was the first one aboard. Riding a cable car was what he most wanted to do.

He led the way to the front section, where the sides were open and the long benches faced out.

Uncle Andy said, "So what do you think, Benny? Is this what you expected?"

"Better!" Benny answered. He had seen pictures of the cable cars. But looking at pictures was not the same as actually riding in one. It was a thrill to rumble and creak up one hill and down another.

"Benny's lucky," Violet said. "He got his wish first."

Andy said, "I didn't pick Benny's paper out of my hat. But he *is* lucky. We can take cable cars to many of the places we'll go."

Benny smiled. He was happy to know this was not his last ride.

The cable car stopped in a park. "End of the line!" the conductor called. The Aldens clambered down the steps.

When everyone had left the cable car, it moved onto a big turntable. The motormen gripped the side rails on the wooden circle and pushed the cable car completely around. Now it was ready for its return trip.

"Wow!" Benny said. "They don't have anything like that in Greenfield!"

Aunt Jane put her arm around his shoulders. "San Francisco is a unique place, all right," she said.

"Let's eat," Uncle Andy said.

Benny smiled. "Aunt Jane's right, Uncle Andy. You are full of good ideas."

They crossed the street to the Buena Vista Café. They sat at a table beside the window and watched people line up for the cable cars. As soon as a car left, another line formed. Along the street, craftsmen sold their wares and musicians played. Beyond, the bay glimmered in the morning light.

"*Buena Vista* means 'beautiful view,'" Aunt Jane told them.

"That's a perfect name," Violet said.

The Aldens and the Beans ate hearty breakfasts of bacon, eggs, toast, and pancakes.

Afterward, they boarded a cable car heading south.

Before long, Uncle Andy said, "This is our stop." They hopped off the car and followed Andy to Grant Street. There they stopped before a tall arch with a green tile roof. Colorful dragon figures decorated the top.

"Henry, I think you'll recognize this," Aunt Jane said.

Henry nodded. "It's the Chinatown Gate."

They passed under the arch into a different world. The narrow streets were crowded with traffic. Colorful signs written in Chinese characters lined the way.

They wandered in and out of shops filled with unusual things. It was hard to resist the hand-carved animals and beautiful clothing. After they had finished shopping, the happy group went down another street into a park. They sat on a bench to rest.

Just then, Violet noticed a young woman across the street. She was coming out of a restaurant. "Isn't that Kate Kerry, the woman who works for Charlie?" she asked.

The other Aldens saw the young woman. She was wearing a yellow slicker with a hood.

"It looks like her," Jessie said, "but I can't tell. She's too far away."

Benny stood up. Waving, he jumped up and down. "Hello! Kate!" he called.

"Benny, don't do that," Jessie said, laughing.

The woman looked toward them. When she did, the hood fell to her shoulders. Her red hair glistened in the sunlight.

"It's her, all right," Benny said. He kept waving.

The woman did not return Benny's greeting. Instead, she hurried around the corner and disappeared.

"That's strange," Benny said. "She didn't even wave."

"I don't think it's strange at all," Jessie said. "She doesn't know us."

Charlie had not introduced them. Benny had forgotten that.

"But she knows *us*," Uncle Andy said.

"Oh, Andy," Aunt Jane said, "she probably didn't see us."

"Maybe it wasn't Kate," Violet suggested. "Jessie is right. She was too far away to tell for sure."

"What about the red hair?" Benny asked.

"A lot of people have hair that color," Violet said.

"Well, she sure did look like Kate," Benny said.

Aunt Jane stood up. "How about lunch? I know the perfect place. Follow me."

A few minutes later, the Aldens entered a crowded restaurant and forgot all about the young woman they had seen. They took seats and looked around.

"Where are the menus?" Jessie asked.

"There are no menus here," Aunt Jane answered.

"How do we order?" Benny asked.

A woman pushed a cart to their table. On it were many small dishes with food on them.

Cart after cart rolled up. The Aldens and

the Beans took some of the small dishes off the carts and sampled everything.

Benny sat back. "I'm full," he said. He noticed a sign. It read DIM SUM. "What does that mean?" he asked.

Uncle Andy shrugged. "Little . . . things."

"I think it means 'little delights' or 'little pleasures,' " Aunt Jane said.

"Whatever it means, it sure tastes good," Benny said.

Violet said, "I've never been to a restaurant that didn't have a menu." She was wondering how they would pay for their lunch. There were no prices listed anywhere.

Uncle Andy seemed to read her mind. "We pay according to the number of empty plates on our table," he explained.

Benny's eyes widened. He began to count the small dishes. When he reached twenty-five, he said, "Wow! This could be expensive!"

But to the Aldens' surprise, the food wasn't expensive at all.

CHAPTER 4

Something Fishy

With the afternoon still ahead of them, they returned to Fisherman's Wharf.

"Let's take a boat ride," Aunt Jane suggested.

"Oh, yes, let's!" Violet said. A boat ride was what she most wanted to do.

"But Violet, it's not your turn," Benny protested. "We didn't pick your paper out of Uncle Andy's hat."

"Your paper wasn't chosen, either," Jessie

reminded him. "But we've already been on the cable cars three times."

"Besides," Henry added, "we're at the wharf. It would make sense to take a boat ride now."

"I guess you're right, Henry," Benny agreed.

Aunt Jane smiled. "You children always work things out," she said proudly.

"There's Charlie," Uncle Andy said. "Let's ask him which boat to take. I'm sure he knows which sightseeing business has the best tours."

Charlie was on the dock beside his boat. When he saw them, he waved.

"He seems friendly today," Benny said.

"The trouble must be over," Violet decided.

Charlie met them on the walkway. "I didn't think I'd see you again so soon," he said.

"We're going to take the children on a boat trip," Aunt Jane told him.

"We thought you'd know which is the best," Uncle Andy added.

"Sightseeing tours?" Charlie said. "That's no way to see the bay. The best way to see it is on a working fishing boat."

"Like yours?" Benny asked. He couldn't imagine anything more fun than a trip on *Charlie's Chum*.

"Like mine," Charlie said. He smiled broadly. "Would you like to come fishing with Kate and me tomorrow morning?"

The Aldens didn't have to think about it. They all said, "Yes!"

"It's hard work," Charlie warned.

"We like work," Benny said.

Just then, Kate Kerry came up to them. She was wearing jeans and a white T-shirt. Her red hair was braided. "Charlie, I have to talk to you," she said. Then she smiled at Aunt Jane and Uncle Andy. "Oh, hello." She looked at the children.

"These are the Aldens," Charlie said.

"They're my brother's grandchildren," Aunt Jane said.

Kate shook hands with each of the children. "Didn't I see you here yesterday?"

"Yes," Violet answered.

"And today!" Benny said. "We saw you today, too."

Kate frowned. "Today? Where?" she asked.

Just as Benny said "Chi — " a tall, dark-haired man ran up.

"Charlie!" he said. "What're you trying to do? Ruin my business?"

Charlie looked flabbergasted. "Vito . . . I . . . I . . ."

"Fresh fish! That's what I need! Not rotten fish!"

"Rotten fish?" Charlie said. "What are you talking about, Vito?"

"Yesterday's order. Half of it was rotten. You think my customers want rotten fish?"

Charlie straightened his shoulders. He stood up tall. "My fish are always fresh," he said. "Always. In all my years, no one has ever complained about my fish."

"Well, I'm complaining," Vito shot back. "And if it ever happens again — "

"Listen here, Mr. Vito Marino, maybe it's *you*," Charlie interrupted. "Maybe you don't know a fresh fish when you smell one."

Vito's mouth dropped open. He seemed to be searching for words. Finally he turned on his heel and stalked off.

"Who was that?" Henry asked.

"Vito Marino," Charlie answered. "He owns a restaurant on the wharf. It's called Vito's Vittles."

"Vito's Vittles," Benny repeated. He thought that was a funny name. He was about to laugh when he saw Henry's warning glance.

"That's what I wanted to talk to you about," Kate said. "Vito's been telling everyone on the wharf that you sold him rotten fish."

"What? That's not true," Charlie said.

Another man joined the group. He was tall and blond. "Great day for fishing, wasn't it?" he asked. Then, noticing Charlie's worried expression, he asked, "What's the problem, Charlie?"

"Oh, Joe," Charlie said. Then he told Joe

about Vito. "Can you believe it?" he concluded. "Me, selling rotten fish?"

Joe shook his head. "Nobody needs this," he said. "If I'd been at it as long as you, Charlie, I'd be thinking of pulling in my nets." Still shaking his head, he wandered off.

"Now, who was that?" Benny asked.

"Joe Martin," Kate answered. "He's a fisherman, too."

"He looks very young," Uncle Andy observed.

"He's new to the business," Charlie said. "But he's a good man. With a little time, he'll be a good fisherman."

Jessie saw someone else — another man — down the way. Although he was dressed casually, she was sure he was the man they had seen lurking here yesterday. She was about to ask if Charlie recognized him when he disappeared behind a building.

"Charlie, perhaps we should wait a day or two before the children go out on your boat," Aunt Jane said.

Charlie looked at her. "Why should we wait?"

"Well, with this trouble and all," Aunt Jane explained. "I just thought that maybe — "

Charlie waved that away. "I'm not the first fisherman to have trouble," he said. "And I won't be the last. Besides, the routine doesn't change." He glanced at the children. "With all this sightseeing, do you think you'll be up to it?" he asked them. "We sail before dawn."

The Aldens looked at Uncle Andy. He would have to drive them to the pier.

"Is that too early, Uncle Andy?" Jessie asked.

Uncle Andy took a deep breath. "Before dawn? That *is* awfully early." He sounded serious, but there was a twinkle in his eyes.

"Oh, you're teasing," Benny said.

Before Uncle Andy had a chance to answer, Kate spoke up. "I have an idea," she said. "Why don't you children stay with me."

Aunt Jane said, "That's nice of you, Kate,

but we wouldn't want to put you to any trouble."

"It's no trouble," Kate assured her. "I'm right over there." She pointed behind her. "It'd be fun having company, and it'd save time in the morning."

Benny was staring off into the distance. "I don't see any houses," he said. "Just boats."

"I live on a boat," Kate said. "That red and white one right down there."

"It doesn't look like a houseboat," Violet said.

"It isn't," Kate said. "It's a sport fishing boat. But there're plenty of bunks. Would you like to stay with me?"

"Oh, yes!" Jessie said. She paused before adding, "If it's all right with Aunt Jane."

Kate said, "Well, Mrs. Bean, what do you say?"

Aunt Jane laughed. "I haven't much choice," she said. "Not with these children. Once they've made up their minds, there's no arguing with them. Just like their grandfather." There was pride in her voice.

"Well, that's settled," Uncle Andy said. "Let's go back home, Jane, and get these new fishermen a change of clothes."

"Give me your packages, children," Aunt Jane said. "We'll take them back home."

The Aldens handed her the things they had bought.

"Bring jackets," Charlie said. "It can get mighty cold out there some mornings."

Kate led the children to her boat. On the way, Violet asked, "Have you lived here long?"

"On and off," Kate answered. "The boat belongs to a friend of mine. He takes out fishing parties. When he's away, he lets me live on the boat."

"Charlie said you're going to college," Henry told her. "What are you studying?"

"Marine biology."

"What's that?" Benny asked.

"It's the science of living things in the sea," Kate explained. She stepped off the dock onto the deck of the boat. "Be careful," she warned the others.

One by one, they jumped onto the deck.

"Look around, make yourselves comfortable," Kate said. "I have to go back to help Charlie."

"May we help, too?" Jessie asked.

Kate shook her head. "Rest up. You'll have plenty of work to do tomorrow." She hopped back onto the dock. "Will you be all right?"

Henry nodded. "We'll be fine. Don't worry about us."

When she was out of sight, Benny said, "We forgot to ask her about Chinatown."

"That wasn't Kate we saw," Violet said.

"What makes you so sure?" Jessie asked.

"Her hair, for one thing. Kate's is braided. That woman's wasn't."

"She could have braided it after we saw her in Chinatown," Jessie said.

That was possible, Violet thought. "But what about the yellow slicker? Kate's not wearing one."

"Maybe it's here," Benny said, heading toward the cabin door.

Jessie called him back. "Don't snoop, Benny."

"Kate said to look around," Benny reminded her.

"She didn't mean we should go through her things," Jessie said.

Sighing, Benny sank into a deck chair.

"It's not important, Benny," Henry said.

"Right," Violet agreed. "And it has nothing to do with the trouble on the wharf."

"I'll bet that man has something to do with it," Jessie said.

Puzzled, the other Aldens looked at her.

"You know — the man we saw yesterday, the man in the suit. He was here again today."

Henry was surprised. "I didn't see him."

"He was in different clothes, but I'm sure it was the same man," Jessie said. "He went behind a building when Joe Martin got close to him."

"Maybe he added the rotten fish to Charlie's catch," Violet suggested.

"Somebody would have seen him do that," Henry said. "Especially yesterday. In that suit, he really stood out. We all noticed him, didn't we?"

"Not me," Benny said. "I didn't see him."

They sat quietly, thinking. The boat rocked gently. Overhead, gulls called to one another.

After a while, Benny began to giggle. "Vito's Vittles," he said. "That is the funniest name for a restaurant." No one else said anything.

Benny paused. Then he said, "What does that word mean: *vittles*?"

"Oh, Benny, you should know that word," Henry said. "It's your favorite thing."

Benny frowned. "My favorite thing?" he said. "Let me see . . ." Slowly, his face relaxed into a big smile. "Oh, I get it. Vittles means food."

Now everyone laughed.

CHAPTER 5

More Trouble

"Aunt Jane and Uncle Andy are already back with our clothes!" Violet said. "Let's go meet them."

She stepped off the boat onto the dock. The other Aldens followed her, excited that they'd be staying on Kate's boat that night.

Their aunt and uncle were visiting with Charlie on the pier near *Charlie's Chum*. Charlie was filling his fuel tank. Kate was checking the fish nets to be sure there were no big tears in them.

"Let's ask Kate about Chinatown," Benny whispered.

"Not now, Benny," Jessie said. "She's busy."

Uncle Andy waved as the children approached.

Aunt Jane held up a duffel bag. "We brought your clothes. Nice warm ones."

A man hurried toward them calling, "Charlie! Charlie!"

Charlie squinted in the man's direction. "That's Tony Gregor," he said. "Looks like more trouble."

"Someone untied my boat!" Tony said. "It floated away!" He gestured toward the bay.

"Who could have done such a thing?" Kate wondered aloud.

The children looked at each other. They thought they knew the answer: the mysterious man in the suit. But they didn't say anything. They had no proof.

"Calm down, Tony," Charlie said.

Tony walked in circles. "I don't know how much longer I can take this."

Charlie put his hand on Tony's shoulder.

Tony stopped his nervous pacing. "What am I going to do?" he asked.

"I'll take you out. We'll get your boat," Charlie said.

Tony seemed relieved. "Thanks, Charlie."

Just then, another boat pulled in beside the narrow pier.

Joe Martin tossed a line over a wooden post. "Hey, Tony, what're you doing here?" he shouted over the sound of the engine. "I just passed your boat on my way in."

That's strange, Henry thought. Earlier, Joe Martin had said he'd had a great day of fishing. Why would he have taken his boat out again? Henry decided not to ask.

Tony told Joe what had happened.

"We were just going out to get it," Charlie said.

"I'll take you, Tony," Joe said. His boat was running, ready to go.

Tony jumped aboard. Joe backed the boat away from the dock and turned it around. Hands on his hips, Charlie stood watching them. His face was creased with worry.

"Say, Charlie," Uncle Andy said, "why don't you come have supper with us. Take your mind off all this."

"Thanks," Charlie responded. "But I couldn't eat. Not now. And I have some work to do."

"How about you, Kate?" Aunt Jane asked.

"I'll stay with Charlie," she answered. She turned to the Aldens. "I'll meet you back here later, okay?"

Aunt Jane left the children's clothes with Kate. Then the Aldens and the Beans walked along the waterfront.

"Is everybody hungry?" Uncle Andy asked.

At first, no one — not even Benny! — was. They were too concerned about the trouble on the wharf to think of food.

Soon, though, the sights and smells along the wharf captured their attention.

"I changed my mind," Benny said. "I'm hungry."

It was such a lovely evening, they decided to eat outside. They bought crab and shrimp cocktails from the outdoor stands and ate them as they strolled near the water.

Far to the west, the sun dropped below the horizon.

"Oh, look!" Jessie said. She pointed toward the Golden Gate Bridge. Its supporting towers stood out against the rosy orange sky.

"What a beautiful sight!" Violet said. She wished she had brought her sketchbook.

Jessie took a deep breath and let it out slowly. "I can't wait to see the bridge up close," she said.

"Maybe we'll go tomorrow after your fishing trip," Aunt Jane told her.

Jessie smiled. That was something to look forward to.

They stopped at Pier 39 for ice-cream cones. Then they headed back toward Charlie's. Aunt Jane and Uncle Andy were in the lead; the Aldens trailed along behind them. Henry stopped suddenly.

"What's the matter, Henry?" Jessie asked.

"I think someone's watching us," he said.

Violet looked over her shoulder. She

quickly turned back. "It's that man again — the one in the suit."

Walking backward, Benny said, "I don't see anyone."

Henry whirled around.

The man was gone.

By the time the Aldens reached the dock, Tony Gregor and Joe Martin had returned.

"Now that everything's shipshape," Charlie said, "I'm going home. I could use a good night's sleep." He turned to Tony. "Do you want a ride?"

Tony shook his head. "I'm staying with my boat tonight," he said. "I don't want it to disappear again."

"That won't happen," Joe assured him. "I'll bet it was an accident. Your knot probably came loose."

Tony glared at him. "My knots never come loose," he said.

Joe shrugged. "Take it easy, Tony. I only meant . . . well, there's always a first time."

Mumbling to himself, Tony headed toward his boat, which was tied to a dock down the way.

Joe watched him. "What did I say?" he asked. Then he smiled at everyone. "Well, I'm off, too. See you in the morning." He ambled away.

Kate picked up the Aldens' duffel bag. "I suppose we should settle in, too," she said.

The Beans hugged their nieces and nephews. "We'll meet you here tomorrow," Aunt Jane told them.

"Be careful," Uncle Andy said.

"Don't worry," Kate said. "I'll keep an eye on them."

The Beans and Charlie headed for their cars.

On Kate's boat, she and the Aldens sat on the open deck. Boat lights bobbed in the dark waters. Overhead, stars shimmered.

"That was too bad about Tony's boat," Benny said. "Do you think it was an accident like Joe said?"

"I doubt it," Kate answered. "There's been too much going on. Someone untied that boat."

"But why?" Jessie asked.

"If Tony lost his boat, he couldn't fish," Violet said.

Kate nodded. "You're right."

"Why would anyone want to keep Tony from fishing?" Henry asked.

Kate shrugged.

"Don't forget the rotten fish," Jessie said. "Vito was really angry. If he quit buying Charlie's fish, what would Charlie do?"

"He'd probably have to quit fishing," Kate answered. "In the old days, there were many more fishermen. The restaurant owners bought all their fish from them. But things have changed. Much of the fish is trucked in from other places. Vito could buy fish from far away."

"It looks as if someone is trying to make all the fishermen quit fishing," Henry concluded.

They fell silent, thinking about the trouble on the wharf.

After a while, Violet yawned. "All this sea air makes me tired."

"And all your sightseeing," Kate added.

That reminded Benny about Chinatown. "Were you sightseeing, too?" he asked Kate.

Kate laughed. "Today? Me? Sightseeing? No way."

"What were you doing in Chinatown, then?"

"I wasn't in Chinatown," Kate said. Then she stood up and stretched. "I think it's about time we turned in."

The Aldens followed her inside the cabin. Bunks lined its sides. A door in the middle opened onto a staircase.

"You take the downstairs," Kate said. "I'll sleep up here."

When the Aldens were tucked into their bunks, Benny said, "She was in Chinatown, all right."

"She said she wasn't," Violet said. "I don't think she would lie."

"She didn't want to talk about it," Benny persisted. "She changed the subject right away."

Henry rolled onto his side. "I don't want to talk about it, either," he said. "I just want to go to sleep." He closed his eyes.

Jessie, Violet, and Benny followed his example.

Henry suddenly remembered something. "Joe said he passed Tony's boat on the way in," he said. "But he docked his boat right after Vito came to complain about the rotten fish. Why would he take his boat out again?"

No one answered him. They were all asleep.

Soon Henry, too, drifted off to sleep.

Later that night, something woke Jessie. She sat up, listening.

Across the room, Henry whispered, "Did you hear that?"

Jessie crept to the window.

Henry followed. "It sounded as if someone had dropped something."

"Look!" Jessie said.

Down the way, a light moved along the dock between Joe's and Charlie's boats.

"That's not a flashlight," Henry observed. "It's flickering."

The light went out.

Jessie and Henry looked at each other. Each had the same question: *Is someone tampering with one of the boats?*

Neither had an answer.

CHAPTER 6

Out to Sea

It was still dark when Kate woke them. "Dress warmly," she said.

The Aldens hurried into their jeans and sweatshirts. They tied their jackets around their waists.

Fruit, juice, and toast awaited them. Kate filled a large thermos. "Hot cocoa," she said. "It tastes really good out there in the fog." She slipped a black poncho over her head and started for the door. "I'll meet you at Charlie's."

When she had gone, Violet said, "You

see, Benny? A black poncho. Not a yellow slicker. We didn't see her yesterday in Chinatown."

"Maybe she has two raincoats," Benny said.

At the door, Henry said, "Let's go. The fish are waiting."

Outside, fog hovered over the water and clung to the docks. Far off, a foghorn blared.

When they reached *Charlie's Chum*, it seemed deserted.

"Where's Kate?" Jessie wondered aloud. "She said she'd meet us here."

Just then, Charlie appeared on deck. His gray hair was tangled and his eyes were sleepy. "Right on time," he said. He stretched and yawned. It looked as if he had just awakened.

Henry said, "I thought you went home last night."

Charlie smoothed his hair with his hands. "I couldn't sleep. Kept thinking something would happen to the boat. So I came back here."

That explained the noise Henry and Jessie had heard and the light they had seen. They were relieved to know there had been no foul play.

Kate ran up to them. "I went to buy some juice," she said and held up a brown paper bag.

When the Aldens were on the boat, Kate untied the rope and hopped aboard. After everyone had put on a life vest, Charlie backed the boat away from the dock and turned it around.

Sea lions barked at them as *Charlie's Chum* passed by on its way out into the bay. Gulls hovered overhead. One gull flew just ahead of them.

"Look!" Benny said. "That bird's leading the way!"

Far off, foghorns sounded. The air was brisk. Before long, the Aldens slipped into their warm jackets. As they neared the Golden Gate Bridge, the water became rough. The boat bumped over the surface.

CHARLIE'S CHUM

"Hang on!" Charlie shouted above the noise of the engine and the sea. The Aldens didn't need to be told.

They passed under the bridge. Jessie looked up, hoping to see the underside of the bridge, but it was too foggy to see much.

In open waters, Charlie slowed the engines. He and Kate lowered the nets into the water.

"What can we do?" Henry asked.

"That's it for now," Kate said. "Just relax and enjoy the ride."

The sun was beginning to burn through the fog. The water glimmered. The boat rose and fell.

In the distance, Henry spotted something. "Look!" he called. "A water spout!"

"Whales," Kate said.

Suddenly a whale broke the surface of the water. As it dove back under, its tail flipped up high in the air.

"Ooohhh!" the Aldens said at once.

"Keep your eyes peeled," Charlie said. "You're apt to see more."

"They're migrating south to warmer waters," Kate added.

Although they looked and looked, that was the only whale they saw.

Later, Charlie reeled in the nets. Fish flipped and flapped on the deck. The Aldens had never seen so many fish.

"These fish have to be sorted according to kind," Kate said.

"That's easy," Henry said.

But, with the fish slipping and sliding, it was more difficult than it looked. Still, they were able to do the job.

"Now put them here," Kate directed. She opened the tops of containers built into the deck. "These are the fish wells."

Charlie turned the boat around. "Time to move to another spot," he said.

By now, the fog had completely lifted. The water sparkled. The sky was clear blue. As they glided nearer to the Golden Gate Bridge, Jessie tilted her head to look up at it. It was so graceful, yet so sturdy. She thought about the people on the bridge. Soon she would be one of them.

Suddenly the engine sputtered and stopped. Kate raced to Charlie's side. "What's wrong?"

"The gauge reads empty," Charlie said. "We're out of fuel."

"You filled the tank last night," Henry said.

"Maybe the gauge is stuck," Jessie suggested.

Charlie tapped the gauge. The needle didn't move.

"Could be a leak." He went to check the tank. It was in good condition. No holes or loose fittings.

"Someone's siphoned off the fuel," Charlie concluded.

"Why would anyone want to do that?" Violet asked

"They wanted us to be stuck out here," Kate answered.

"But no one was near your boat last night until you came back," Henry said.

"Yes," Jessie added. "We saw your light."

Charlie looked surprised. "Light? I didn't use a light. I know this wharf like the back of my hand. I don't need a light. A little moonlight's all I need."

"Then someone *was* at the dock last night!" Henry concluded.

Benny wasn't listening. He was squinting toward shore. "How're we going to get back?" he said, his voice trembling a little.

Kate put an arm around his shoulders and pulled him close. "Don't worry, Benny. We'll call the Coast Guard on the radio. They'll come get us." She went inside the cabin.

Benny relaxed. "Good thing you have a radio, Charlie," he said.

"We couldn't go out without one," Charlie told him. "We never know when we'll need help."

Kate came back outside. They looked at her expectantly. "The radio's not working," she said. "One of the wires has been cut."

Violet's eyes grew wide. "We're stuck out here," she said.

"We're drifting farther away from the bridge!" Jessie said.

Then they heard a splash. Charlie had dropped the anchor.

"Now we won't go anywhere," he said. "We'll just sit here and wait. Someone will see us and come to help."

They sat for a long time. No one came to help.

Finally Henry saw a sailboat. It seemed to be coming their way. "Violet, quick! Give me your jacket," he said.

Violet handed him her pale lavender windbreaker.

"Your jacket is the lightest color," he explained. "Maybe they'll see it." He waved it above his head.

The boat moved farther away.

"It's going the other way," Jessie said. Disappointed, Henry lowered the jacket.

"I might have a flare," Charlie said, and he went inside the cabin to look. The others searched for something they could use to attract attention.

"Ahoy there!" someone called.

Benny ran to the rail. "It's Joe!"

Sure enough: Joe Martin's boat was

moving toward them. They all waved and shouted.

Joe cut his engine and drifted in. "What's the trouble?"

"We've run out of gas!" Benny shouted.

"And the radio's dead," Kate added.

"I'll go ashore and bring back some fuel," Joe offered.

"Can you take the children with you?" Charlie asked.

"Sure thing." Joe threw a line onto Charlie's boat. Kate caught it.

The boats were pulled side by side. "Benny, you go first," Henry directed.

"Watch your step," Joe said. He reached out his hand.

The boats pitched and rolled. When one bobbed up, the other dropped down.

This was not going to be easy. Benny took a deep breath. He grabbed hold of Joe's hand.

"Gotcha!" Joe said as Benny jumped into his arms.

Soon the other Aldens were aboard Joe's boat. Kate and Charlie stayed behind.

"I'll be back soon," Joe said as he nosed his boat away from *Charlie's Chum*.

"Lucky you were out here," Henry commented.

Joe smiled. "I was just coming in."

"Do you go out fishing more than once a day?" Henry asked.

Joe's smile faded. "No. Why?"

"Well, you went out twice yesterday," Henry said.

For a moment Joe looked confused. Then he smiled again. "Oh, yeah, right. When I brought in my catch, I noticed the engine seemed sluggish. I took her out later to check. That's when I saw Tony's boat."

"The engine seems fine now," Jessie said.

Joe nodded. "Probably my imagination."

Before long, the Aldens were back on shore. They waited on the pier for Charlie and Kate.

"Who do you suppose took the fuel?" Jessie asked.

Henry shrugged. "It was the person we saw last night. That's the only thing I'm sure of."

Violet and Benny said, "What person?"

Henry explained about the noise and the light he and Jessie had seen. "But it was too dark to tell who it was," he concluded.

"This morning we thought it was Charlie returning to his boat," Jessie said. "But then he told us that he didn't use a light."

"Maybe it was that mysterious man you keep seeing," Benny teased. He hadn't seen the man and wasn't sure he really existed.

Soon Charlie swung his boat up to the dock. Henry caught Charlie's line and tied it to a post. Kate and Charlie hopped onto the deck as Vito Marino trotted up.

"How was your catch?" he asked Charlie. "The restaurant is completely booked for tonight."

"We had a little trouble," Charlie said. "It shortened our day. I'll bring you our catch as soon as I prepare it."

"Show it to me now!" Vito insisted.

Charlie swung back aboard. Vito followed him. In no time, Vito was back on the dock, complaining.

"You can't say they aren't fresh," Charlie told him.

"They might be fresh, but there aren't enough of them to fill tonight's dinner orders," Vito snapped. "I'm telling you, Charlie, I can't deal with this." He stormed off.

Tony and Joe came up to find out what was happening. Kate explained.

"If anything else happens, I'll lose the account," Charlie said.

Joe's face clouded. "That's too bad, Charlie. That's a good account. Vito's is popular. He uses lots of fish."

Tony nodded. "I'd give anything if Vito would buy fish from me."

They all returned to prepare their boats for the next day. The Aldens waited nearby for Aunt Jane and Uncle Andy.

"Do you suppose Joe or Tony is causing the trouble?" Violet asked.

"They each have a motive," Henry said. "If Vito doesn't buy from Charlie, he might buy from one of them."

"It can't be Joe," Violet said. "He's too nice."

"Right," Benny agreed. "He took Tony out to get his boat, and he rescued us. Guilty people aren't *that* nice."

"Tony can't be the one," Jessie said. "Someone let his boat go. He wouldn't do that himself."

"He might have done it so no one would suspect him," Violet suggested.

"Or maybe Joe was right: Tony's knot came undone and the boat just drifted away," Benny said.

"Tony *was* on the wharf last night," Henry said. "He slept on his boat, remember? He could've sneaked onto the *Chum* before Charlie came back here."

"And he did say he'd give anything if Vito would buy fish from him," Jessie said.

Benny nodded. "He probably took the gas and broke the radio."

"There's that strange man," Henry said.

"Maybe he has nothing to do with the trouble, Henry," Violet said. "Just because he hangs around the wharf doesn't mean — "

"No, no," Henry interrupted. "I mean: *There he is!*"

They followed his gaze. The man stood against a wooden shack at the other end of the wharf. His sunglasses glinted in the light.

This time everyone — even Benny — saw him.

CHAPTER 7

Another Sighting

"What are you looking at?" a voice asked.

It was Aunt Jane.

"We keep seeing that man," Henry explained. "We've been thinking he might have something to do with the trouble."

Aunt Jane looked around. "What man?"

Jessie said, "He's over there."

But he wasn't. He had disappeared again.

"You children shouldn't worry about these things," Aunt Jane said. "Let Charlie and the other fishermen take care of it."

"But we're very good detectives," Benny said. "We've had lots of experience."

"Even detectives need time off, Benny," Aunt Jane said. She held up a bag. "I've brought lunch," she told them.

After the morning's fishing, they were all hungry.

"Where's Uncle Andy?" Jessie asked.

"Working," she answered. "After lunch, we'll take the ferry to Sausalito. Uncle Andy will meet us there later, and we'll drive home across the Golden Gate Bridge."

Jessie was especially happy to hear that. "Sounds great!" she said.

"There's Kate!" Henry said.

Waving, Kate headed their way.

"Let's ask her if she wants to go to Sausalito with us," Aunt Jane suggested. The Aldens liked that idea.

Kate couldn't go. "I have studying to do," she said. "But I have an invitation for you. Charlie wants you to come fishing tomorrow. He feels you were cheated today because of the trouble."

"May we go, Aunt Jane?" Jessie asked.

"I don't see why not," Aunt Jane said.

"And you can stay with me again," Kate said.

"Oh, but if you have studying to do . . ." Aunt Jane objected.

"I have all afternoon to study," Kate assured her.

"Well, okay, then. It's nice of you to ask, Kate," Aunt Jane said.

Benny hopped on one foot. "Oh, good! We can stay!"

"I'll meet you back here later," Kate said, and hurried away.

Aunt Jane and the children found a bench near the water. They ate peanut butter sandwiches, homemade chocolate chip cookies, and milk. Terns and gulls hovered overhead. When Benny dropped a bit of bread, one swooped in and caught it before it touched the ground.

Violet squinted, looking across the water. "Where is Sausalito?"

Aunt Jane pointed out a hill across the bay. "It's only a twenty-minute ferry ride," she said.

Henry collected the trash and dropped it into a can. "Are we ready?" he asked.

They walked along the waterfront to the ferry landing. "Looks like we just missed a ferry," Jessie said.

"They run often," Aunt Jane told her.

Waiting there, where the scenery was so beautiful, did not seem like waiting at all. Before long, a line formed behind them. Soon another boat was ready to make the trip.

Benny was the first down the long ramp. "Can we go to the top?" he asked.

"You children run along," Aunt Jane said. "I'm going to stay inside out of the wind."

The children clambered up the narrow stairway. "Be careful," Aunt Jane called after them.

They took positions along the upper rail. As they cruised across the bay, Violet pointed out a small island. Atop it was a big building. "What's that?" she asked.

"Alcatraz," Henry told her.

"What a funny name," Benny said.

Henry had read about the island. He

knew its history. "In the beginning, no one lived there but pelicans."

"Look!" Violet said. "There're some now!" Sure enough, squat, brown pelicans floated nearby.

"That's how it got its name," Henry continued. "*Alcatraces* means 'pelicans' in Spanish. A long time ago, soldiers were stationed there. Later, it became a prison."

Benny pulled his jacket tight around him. "A cold and windy prison," he said.

Jessie pointed to a hill ahead. There were colorful houses on its steep slope. "That must be Sausalito," she said.

The ferry nosed into the dock. Aunt Jane was waiting on the lower deck. They all followed the crowd onto the ramp. People were lined up, waiting for the return trip.

"There's Uncle Andy!" Aunt Jane said. "He must have finished his work early." She went on ahead to meet her husband.

Violet noticed a man and woman huddled together talking. She poked Henry. "There's that strange man again," she whispered.

"And there's Kate!" Benny blurted. He was so surprised to see Kate in a yellow slicker, he didn't think to keep his voice quiet.

Jessie studied the two people. The girl had her hood up and was turned away. Jessie couldn't tell whether or not it was Kate. But she was sure the man was the one they kept seeing on Fisherman's Wharf.

"I'm going to try to get a look at that woman," Henry said. He threaded his way through the crowd. But it was too late. The woman and the man had already boarded the ferry.

"That was Kate, all right," Benny said.

"We can't be certain, Benny," Jessica said.

"She said she was going to study," Violet reminded her little brother.

"Suppose it *was* Kate," Henry said. "Why would she be meeting that man?"

"Maybe she and the man are causing all the trouble," Benny suggested. "They met to plan more bad stuff."

"But why would she meet him *here*?"

Jessie wondered aloud. "She knew we were coming."

Uncle Andy waved and called to them. "Hurry up, slowpokes!"

The Aldens quickened their pace. "Let's give this some thought," Henry said. "We'll talk about it later."

Uncle Andy and Aunt Jane led them to the main street. "This street is called Bridgeway," Uncle Andy said.

Lots of interesting shops were clustered along one side. Across the way, two elephant statues marked the entrance to a park. Beyond, yachts rocked in the blue waters of the marina.

"What does Sausalito mean?" Violet asked.

"*Sauces* in Spanish means 'willow trees,' " Uncle Andy explained.

"And *lito* means 'little,' " Henry said.

Benny looked around. "I don't see any willow trees," he said.

Uncle Andy laughed. "They must be here somewhere."

After a while, Benny said, "All this walking makes me — "

"Hungry," everyone else finished.

"Then it's time to go back," Aunt Jane said.

Uncle Andy led them to his car. "I thought you might like to eat dinner at Vito's."

"Vito's Vittles," Benny said, chuckling to himself.

Uncle Andy drove out of Sausalito to the main road. They rode through a tunnel and then they were on the Golden Gate Bridge.

Jessie didn't know where to look. To the west, the sun spread a golden path on the water. To the east, San Francisco was outlined against the brilliant sky. Straight ahead, the orange towers of the bridge rose high above them.

"Well, Jessie," Uncle Andy asked, "is it what you expected?"

"Much more," Jessie answered.

Back at the wharf, they parked and headed toward the restaurant.

On their way, they passed the docks. Kate and Charlie were on *Charlie's Chum*. Kate was not wearing a yellow slicker.

"How about dinner?" Uncle Andy called to them.

Charlie said, "Not tonight, thanks."

"I'd better help Charlie," Kate said.

But Charlie wouldn't hear of it. "You go along. I'm about finished here."

Kate joined them. "I am hungry," she said.

"Did you finish your studying?" Jessie asked.

"Every bit of it," Kate answered. "Seems I know more than I thought I did." She smiled broadly and looked them in the eye. Either she wasn't the person they had seen in Sausalito or she was a very good liar.

The restaurant was bustling with activity. Vito greeted them at the door. "I have the perfect table for you," he said, and he led them to a round table that looked out on the harbor. He handed menus all around.

"I suppose we shouldn't order fish," Henry said.

"Why not, Henry?" Aunt Jane asked.

Before Henry could answer, Vito said, "Not order fish? Vito's is known for its fish. What do you want? The catch of the day? Salmon? Tuna? Sea bass? You name it; I have it." Then he quickly walked away.

"That's strange," Jessie said.

"What is this about?" Uncle Andy asked.

"We ran out of fuel this morning," Kate explained, "and we had to cut the fishing short."

"And Vito told Charlie he wouldn't have enough fish for tonight's dinner," Henry concluded.

"Vito was really angry," Benny added.

Uncle Andy shrugged. "He seems to have all the fish he needs."

"Maybe he bought some from someone else," Violet suggested. Everyone sat and thought about the mystery.

Finally they opened their menus. They had a difficult time making a selection. Everything sounded so good. Each of them decided to order something different. That way they could sample many dishes.

Benny looked around the restaurant. Old anchors, wheels, and other boat gear hung on the walls. The window in the kitchen door was a round porthole.

Suddenly Benny pulled at Henry's sleeve. "There's that man again!" he muttered. Henry looked up in time to see the mysterious man at the round window. Jessie and Violet saw him, too.

The Aldens exchanged puzzled glances. Each wondered the same thing: *What is that man doing in the kitchen of Vito's Vittles?*

CHAPTER 8

Sounds in the Night

After dinner, Henry, Jessie, Violet, and Benny went back to Kate's boat. While they were relaxing on the boat deck, it began to rain.

"We should go inside," Kate said.

"But it isn't raining hard," Jessie said. "May we stay up here for a little bit longer?"

"Okay. I'll get your jackets," Kate said. When she came back with them, the children put on their jackets and Kate slipped into her black poncho.

"Do you have a yellow slicker?" Violet asked.

Kate looked at her. "A yellow slicker? No. Why?"

Violet's face reddened. "Oh . . . uh . . ."

"Yellow is Violet's favorite color," Benny piped up. "Next to purple."

It began to pour. "I guess it's time to turn in," Kate said.

Once the Aldens were settled for the night, they discussed the events of the day.

"Do you suppose Vito is in on this?" Jessie asked.

"Why would Vito be causing trouble for the fishermen?" Henry said. "He needs their fish."

"I don't know," Jessie said. "It just seemed odd seeing that mysterious man in Vito's kitchen."

"That's right," Violet said. "What was he doing there?"

"Maybe he's the one who sold fish to Vito," Benny suggested.

"I don't think he's a fisherman," Violet said. "Where would he get the fish?"

They all thought about that. Finally Jessie said, "Maybe he works for one of the fishermen."

"That's possible," Henry agreed. "He could be helping to ruin Charlie's business so Vito will buy from someone else."

"What about Kate?" Benny asked. "What was she doing in Sausalito with that man?"

"That wasn't Kate," Violet argued. "You heard her say she doesn't own a yellow slicker."

"Well, it *was* Kate we saw in Chinatown," Benny said.

"We can't be sure, Benny," Jessie said.

"What about the red hair?" Benny persisted.

After a silence, Violet said, "Benny, there are lots of people with hair like that. And San Francisco is a big city."

Jessie yawned. "This is getting way too complicated," she said.

* * *

Late that night, Benny awoke with a start. "What was that?" he whispered. There it was again: the noise that had awakened him.

At the window, Henry said, "I think someone's on Charlie's dock."

Beside him, Jessie murmured, "Someone is out there. See that light?"

Violet and Benny crept out of bed. Before they could reach the window, another sound cut through the silence.

Breaking glass!

"What's happening?" Benny asked.

"The light went out," Henry told him.

Jessie peered through the window. "I don't see anyone."

"It's too dark out there," Henry said as he returned to bed. "And we don't know our way around the dock very well. Let's check it out in the morning."

Benny climbed under the covers. "Maybe Charlie came back to sleep on the boat again."

"Charlie doesn't use a light," Henry reminded him.

"Maybe he needed one tonight," Violet said. "There's no moon."

"We'll have to wait until morning to find out," Jessie said.

The next morning, they awoke to the sound of foghorns.

Henry looked at the clock. "It's late," he said. "We'd better get moving."

They dressed quickly.

"I wonder if Kate's still sleeping," Violet said.

In the main cabin, Jessie had the answer. "She isn't here."

They went outside on the deck to look for her. She wasn't there, either. In the distance, a patch of yellow shone through the drifting fog.

Violet squinted through the haze. "Look!" she said. "It's the woman in the yellow slicker."

"And she's on Joe Martin's boat!" Jessie added.

Benny nodded. "It's Kate," he said. "She's in on this with Joe Martin."

"Let's go," Henry urged. "We'll see what she's up to."

They hurried inside, grabbed their jackets, dashed back outside, and hopped onto the dock. Then they raced along the walkway to Charlie's and Joe's pier.

The red-haired woman was gone!

"We should tell Charlie about Kate," Benny said.

"Tell him what?" Henry asked.

"That she and Joe Martin and that strange man are causing all the trouble," Benny answered.

"But we don't know for sure, Benny," Jessie said.

"Charlie would never believe us," Henry added.

"*I* don't even believe it," Violet said.

"Yoo-hoo!" someone called.

It was Kate. She hurried toward them.

"She's not wearing the yellow slicker," Violet observed.

"Maybe we *didn't* see her on Joe's boat," Violet said. "Maybe we didn't see anyone. Maybe it was a trick of the fog."

Kate came up beside them. She was carrying a shopping bag. "I bought sourdough bread — a San Francisco specialty — for our breakfast," she said. "And lots of good snacks for later."

From his boat, Charlie called, "Are you landlubbers ready to set sail?"

"What's a landlubber?" Benny whispered.

Henry answered, "Someone who lives on the land and doesn't know much about the sea."

Benny chuckled. "That's us."

Kate led the parade to the boat. Waiting his turn to board, Henry saw something glistening on the dock. He leaned over and picked it up. It was a piece of broken glass.

"Come on, Henry," Charlie urged him. "The fish are waiting."

Henry set the glass fragment on top of a barrel where no one would step on it. Then he hopped aboard.

"Is the radio fixed?" Violet asked. She didn't want to be stuck out in the water again.

"Fixed," Charlie said. "Everything's ship-shape." Charlie backed the *Chum* away from the dock. "This is going to be a good day. I can feel it in my bones."

The Aldens hoped he was right.

CHAPTER 9

The Fish That Got Away

It was a perfect day — even more beautiful than the day before had been. The sea was calm. The sky was bright. The fishing was good.

It was difficult to think about trouble on a day like this.

"You were right," Benny said to Charlie. "This *is* a very good day."

Even the birds knew it. They hovered over the boat, squawking. Benny and Violet tore bits of bread from the large loaf Kate had brought and tossed them to the gulls. The birds dipped and dived, snatching up the tidbits.

They were having such a good time that when Charlie said "Let's haul in the nets," they were disappointed.

"Are we going in already?" Benny asked.

Kate smiled. "No, Benny," she said. "But the nets are full. We'll empty them into the well and cast them out again."

Kate and the Aldens helped reel in the nets. Charlie whistled as they worked. Fish jumped and splashed. Many of them escaped to slip back into the cold waters.

"They're getting away!" Violet said.

"Don't worry," Charlie told her. "We have plenty to spare."

And then the nets were up out of the water.

Empty!

Charlie's mouth dropped open. Kate gasped. The Aldens stared in disbelief. But it was true. Except for the few fish that had gotten tangled, the nets were empty. Char-

lie ran his hands along the netting. He punched his fist through one large rip after another.

"This can't be," Kate said. "I checked those nets myself."

Charlie was too angry to speak. He turned the boat around and headed for shore. Kate and the Aldens kept silent, too.

Ashore, the word spread quickly. Before long, Vito Marino stormed onto the dock. "Is it true?" he demanded. "Did you come in empty, Charlie?"

Charlie looked at him long and hard. Then he turned away without answering.

"It's true," Kate said.

"This is the last straw," Vito said. "I'm sorry, Charlie, but I can't depend on you."

Joe Martin's boat eased up to the dock. "What's going on?" he asked as he threw a line over a post. Kate told him.

Joe hopped onto the deck beside Charlie. "Oh, Charlie, what bad luck." He turned to Vito. "I had a very good day. Maybe I could help out until Charlie gets back on his feet."

He ushered Vito onto his boat for a look at the catch.

Vito shook Joe's hand. "It's a deal, Joe," he said. "I'll buy your fish."

Charlie watched them silently with narrowed eyes.

"Don't let this get you down, Charlie," Kate said. "Come on. Let's repair the nets."

Charlie waved her away. "It's no use," he said. "I'm finished." With hunched shoulders and slow steps, he headed off the pier.

"Let's go after him," Benny murmured. "We can tell him what we know."

Henry held him back. "We have to think about this first."

Kate came up beside them. "I'm going after Charlie," she told him. "Will you be all right?"

Jessie nodded. "We'll be fine. You go ahead." Kate trotted away.

"Joe and Kate," Benny said. "They're the ones."

Violet looked sad. "I can't believe Kate has anything to do with this."

"She could have cut the nets this morning," Henry said.

"Or last night," Jessie said. "She might have been the person we heard."

Henry nodded. "She had plenty of chances. She could have siphoned the gas and cut the radio wire, too."

Jessie agreed. "No one would suspect anything if they saw her on Charlie's boat."

"If she *is* working with Joe, it would all make sense," Henry said. "Joe wanted Vito's business; she helped him get it."

"But what about Tony?" Violet asked. "He said he'd give anything to get Vito's business. And don't forget Vito and that strange man. Maybe they were planning all this last night in the restaurant kitchen."

Benny nodded. "All of them — they're all in on it."

"We have to tell Charlie," Jessie said.

Henry shook his head. "He'll never believe us — not without proof."

"Well, then, let's get some," Benny suggested.

"We'll start right here," Henry said. He

began walking along Charlie's and Joe's dock. "Look for anything strange," he directed the others. "Anything that looks out of place."

Jessie and Violet stepped onto *Charlie's Chum*. They poked in boxes and peered under seats. On the pier, Henry moved alongside the boat, his eyes downcast. He found nothing but the glass fragment he had seen that morning.

Across from him, Benny examined Joe's side of the dock. "There's nothing here," Benny said at last. Then he noticed something inside a coil of rope. "Oh, wait." He pulled the rope aside. "Forget it," he said. "It's just an old lantern like the one we use when we go camping."

"Let's walk along the wharf," Jessie suggested. "We might find some clue there." But they found nothing.

Finally Henry said, "Proof or no proof, I think we have to tell Charlie what we think."

"But you said he won't believe us," Violet reminded him.

"We'll have to convince him," Henry said.

"Maybe he can put the puzzle together," Jessie added.

Thinking Charlie might have returned to the boat, they doubled back. He wasn't there.

"Let's go get some lunch. We can talk more about what we know," Henry said. They decided to go to Pier 39.

When they were nearly there, they stopped short. Ahead of them, at the pier entrance, two men stood talking.

One of the men was Charlie. The other was the mysterious man! The Aldens ducked around a corner so Charlie wouldn't see them.

"What could Charlie be talking to that man about?" Benny wondered aloud.

"Maybe he found out the man has something to do with all the trouble," Violet suggested, "and he's telling him to stop."

"That's possible," Henry said.

"It's also possible that Charlie is *part* of the problem," Jessie said.

"Charlie?" Violet sounded surprised. "But most of the bad things have been happening to *him*."

No one could deny that.

"Well, one thing is sure," Henry said. "We can't tell Charlie what we suspect. Not now. Not until we know more."

"We'll keep looking for proof after we eat," Jessie said.

They ordered pizza in one of the many pier restaurants. Waiting for their order, each Alden was silent, thinking.

"I wonder where Tony was," Jessie said at last.

"When?" Henry asked.

"Just now when we came back to shore."

"He's probably still out fishing," Violet suggested.

"But every other time there was trouble, he was there," Jessie reminded them. "Joe, Vito, Tony — they were all there."

Benny's eyes widened. "Maybe he cut the nets, and he didn't want to be around when Charlie found out."

"But if he did it to get Vito's business,

he'd want to be there when Vito came along," Jessie said.

"That's right," Violet said. "Joe was there, so he got the business."

The pizza arrived. For a while, they were too busy eating to talk. When they had nearly finished, Henry said, "We should stop thinking and talking about the trouble on the wharf."

"Why?" Benny wanted to know.

"You can think about something too hard," Henry explained. "Sometimes, if you put a problem in the back of your mind, the answer just . . . pops up."

"Oh, I get it," Benny said. "It's there all the time, but you can't see it."

They all thought Henry might be right.

"But if we don't talk about the mystery," Benny said, "what should we talk about?"

"About the things we still want to see," Henry answered. He pulled the rolled guidebook from his back pocket. "There are so many interesting places in San Francisco. We've only been to a few."

"Golden Gate Park is something we should see," Jessie said.

Henry agreed. "That's one I've marked. Especially the Academy of Sciences. There's a planetarium there and an aquarium."

"More *fish*?" Benny said. "Haven't we seen enough of those?"

"They have a Touch Tide Pool, Benny, where you can actually hold starfish and sea urchins." He opened the book and read aloud from it.

"The Japanese Tea Gardens sound interesting," Violet said.

"We could spend the whole day in the park," Jessie said. "There's so much to see. We'll make a list and give it to Uncle Andy," she decided.

CHAPTER 10

The Catch of the Day

When they returned to the docks, the Aldens met Kate.

"I've been looking for you," she said. "Your aunt phoned. She and your uncle will be late. They don't expect to get here until dinnertime. I wish I had time to take you sightseeing, but with Charlie and all . . ." Her voice trailed off.

"We'll find plenty to do," Jessie assured her.

"How *is* Charlie?" Henry asked.

Kate shrugged. "He wanted to be alone,"

she said. Her green eyes were sad.

"Alone?" Benny repeated. "But we just saw him with — "

Jessie gave him a poke.

"It's not at all like him," Kate continued. "I'm going to find him now and try to talk to him. See you later," she said, and started away.

Kate could not be involved in the trouble. She was too nice, too concerned about other people. The person they had seen in Chinatown, Sausalito, and on Joe Martin's boat wasn't Kate. Violet was sure of it.

"She didn't do it," Violet murmured.

Benny didn't like to see Violet upset. To make her feel better, he said, "If Kate did do it, she probably had a really good reason."

But it didn't work. "You all think she's guilty," Violet said. "And now you think Charlie's in on it, too."

"We don't know for sure," Jessie said. "We're just trying to figure it out."

Henry put an arm around Violet's shoulders. "We hope Kate and Charlie have nothing to do with all this," he said. "We hope nobody we know is involved."

"Yes," Jessie added. "Joe and Tony — they're good people, too. It's hard to believe either of them could be guilty."

Even Violet had to agree that was true.

"If we knew more about the mysterious man," Henry said, "we might be able to solve this puzzle."

They decided to look for the man.

"What will we do if we find him?" Benny asked.

"We'll decide that when the time comes," Jessie answered.

The time never came. They looked all over the piers, but they could not find the mysterious man.

Just before sunset, they gathered on the wharf. Charlie was himself again, friendly and positive. He and Kate were repairing the torn nets.

The Aldens wondered if his good mood

might have had something to do with his meeting with the mysterious man earlier in the day.

Tony Gregor was helping Kate and Charlie. *If he had cut the nets, why would he help repair them?* Henry wondered.

"Has anyone seen Joe?" Tony asked.

Charlie shrugged. "Not since he brought in his catch."

"Perfect timing, too," Kate added, "with Vito ready to buy."

"Here comes Joe," Benny said.

Joe Martin sauntered toward them, a big smile on his face.

Looking at him, the Aldens thought it was hard to believe that he had anything to do with the trouble on the wharf. He had helped Tony rescue his boat; he had brought the Aldens to shore when they were stranded; and he had returned to the *Chum* with fuel. And, even today, when he sold Vito his catch, he had said, "Maybe I could help out until Charlie gets back on his feet." That didn't sound like a man who was trying to steal Charlie's business.

"Hey, there," Joe said. "This looks like a party."

"It's a repair-the-torn-net party," Charlie said. "Want to help?"

Joe's smile faded. "Wish I could," he said, "but I have some work of my own." He went down the dock to his boat and disappeared inside. A few minutes later, he was back. "Charlie, do you have a lantern I could borrow? It's getting too dark to work without one, and I can't find mine."

Benny remembered the lantern in the coil of rope. He said, "But we saw — "

Henry remembered the lantern, too. "I'll get you a light," he interrupted, and dashed away.

"Do you know where my lantern is?" Charlie called after Henry.

"Don't worry, Charlie," Benny said. "He'll find a light."

Henry was back in a flash, carrying a lantern.

"That's not my lantern," Charlie said.

"I think Joe knows who owns it," Henry said. He held up a piece of broken glass.

"And I think he knows who owns this, too." He turned the lantern to reveal a hole the shape of the broken glass.

Joe's smile froze. "I . . . uh . . . "

"We heard glass breaking out on the dock last night," Violet said.

Charlie glared at Joe. "So you were the one who ripped these nets."

Joe backed away. "No, no. Not me. I didn't do it."

"And you siphoned off our fuel and broke the radio," Kate said.

"No, listen," Joe pleaded. "I didn't do any of those things. I *did* break my lantern. I came back here last night to check on my boat. I tripped over something and the lantern fell."

Jessie said, "But you said you couldn't find your lantern."

Joe seemed to be searching for a reply. Finally he said, "I . . . uh . . . I was embarrassed. What kind of fisherman breaks his lantern?"

"A greedy fisherman." The words came from behind them.

The Aldens whirled around.

The voice belonged to Kate!

That couldn't be. Kate was beside them. Yet the faces were the same; the red hair was the same. But this woman wore a yellow slicker.

"Two Kates!" Benny exclaimed.

Kate was no less surprised. "Kim!" she cried. "What are you doing here?"

The other woman said, "Before I tell you that, let me introduce Sam Goodall." She gestured toward the man beside her.

The mysterious man!

"He's an investigator," Kim continued.

Sam Goodall stepped forward. "Some of the fishermen hired me to find out who was causing the trouble on the wharf," he explained. "I suspected you, Joe, from the beginning, but I could never find the proof." He turned to the Aldens. "The lantern is just what I needed to close this case, and I have you kids to thank for that."

Joe Martin raised his arms into the air. "All right," he said. "I did it. I didn't mean to ruin anyone's business. I just wanted to show that I could be as good as the other fishermen. But how could I compete with men like Charlie and Tony?"

"It takes years of practice," Kate told him. "You've only just started."

Sam Goodall glanced at Charlie and Tony. "What do you want to do about this?"

"Joe should pay for what he's done," Tony said.

Charlie thought about that. "Joe has the makings of a good fisherman," he said. "But he has to learn to have patience. If he works for us for a while, we can teach him. And he'll be making up for our losses at the same time. What do you think, Tony?"

"Great idea, Charlie," Tony answered. "I think the other fishermen will agree."

Then Sam took Joe aside to ask him a few more questions.

Now only one mystery remained: Who was the young woman in the yellow slicker?

Kate answered that question. "This is my

twin sister, Kim," she said. "She's studying to be a private investigator."

"I'm very happy to meet you, Kim," Violet said, and then she looked at her brothers and sister. Her expression said, *I told you so.*

"She'll have to tell you what she's doing here," Kate continued, "because I haven't the slightest idea."

"Sam asked me to help out," Kim explained. "I took a job delivering fish for Joe. That way I could keep an eye on him."

"But why didn't you tell me?" Kate asked.

"I asked her not to," Sam answered. "The fewer people who knew, the better."

"Believe me, Kate," Kim said, "it wasn't easy. I *wanted* to tell you. Talk about patience!"

"But Joe must've known you were Kate's twin," Charlie said. "And he never mentioned it."

"I asked him not to," Kim explained. "I told him Kate and I were having some problems and she'd be upset if she knew I was working down here."

"Were you delivering fish in Chinatown?" Henry asked.

Kim nodded. "Joe has been supplying one of the restaurants there."

"What about Sausalito?" Violet asked.

Kim looked surprised. "You saw me in Sausalito?"

"Yes," Benny answered. "But we thought you were Kate."

"*I* didn't think so," Violet said.

Kim nodded. "I was delivering fish there, too."

"We saw *you* there, too," Benny told Sam.

"I decided to go along," Sam said. "It gave us the chance to exchange information. We couldn't risk being seen together. We figured no one would see us there."

"But you were wrong," Benny piped up.

Sam laughed. "We didn't know you were such good detectives."

"We've had lots of practice," Benny said.

Vito Marino came running toward them. "I just heard about Joe. Is it true?"

Charlie explained what had happened. Vito was upset. "What are we going to do about this?" he asked.

"We're going to teach Joe the importance of honesty," Tony said.

Shortly thereafter, Aunt Jane and Uncle Andy arrived.

"Is everyone ready for dinner?" Aunt Jane asked.

"We sure are," Benny answered.

Vito said, "Come to my place. Dinner's on me." He turned to Joe. "You're not charging me for those fish you brought in this morning, are you, Joe?"

Joe shook his head. "No. They're my gift to you," he mumbled. "It's the least I can do."

Kate introduced the Beans to her sister, Kim, and to Sam Goodall. Then everyone — except Joe, who stayed behind to repair the nets — headed for Vito's Vittles. On the way there, the Aldens excitedly discussed the events of the day.

In the distance, the sky was a brilliant red. The lights on the Golden Gate Bridge looked like bright beads strung across the bay. This was truly a beautiful city. And there was so much of it left to see.

"So, Vito, what's the catch of the day?" Uncle Andy asked.

The Aldens smiled at one another. They had just helped uncover a troublemaker. That was the real catch of the day.

Laughing, Jessie said, "It was a big one, Uncle Andy. A really big one!"

GERTRUDE CHANDLER WARNER discovered when she was teaching that many readers who like an exciting story could find no books that were both easy and fun to read. She decided to try to meet this need, and her first book, *The Boxcar Children*, quickly proved she had succeeded.

Miss Warner drew on her own experiences to write the mystery. As a child she spent hours watching trains go by on the tracks opposite her family home. She often dreamed about what it would be like to set up housekeeping in a caboose or freight car — the situation the Alden children find themselves in.

When Miss Warner received requests for more adventures involving Henry, Jessie, Violet, and Benny Alden, she began additional stories. In each, she chose a special setting and introduced unusual or eccentric characters who liked the unpredictable.

While the mystery element is central to each of Miss Warner's books, she never thought of them as strictly juvenile mysteries. She liked to stress the Aldens' independence and resourcefulness and their solid New England devotion to using up and making do. The Aldens go about most of their adventures with as little adult supervision as possible — something else that delights young readers.

Miss Warner lived in Putnam, Connecticut, until her death in 1979. During her lifetime, she received hundreds of letters from girls and boys telling her how much they liked her books.